Meet the
Barkers

MORGAN AND MOFFAT GO TO SCHOOL

Written and illustrated by

TOMIE dePAOLA

G. P. Putnam's Sons ★ New York

For Madison, Moffat, Morgan, Markus, Mario & Fey;
Bingley & Bob; and of course, Jenny, Tony & Fraser—
and everyone else who loves Welsh terriers.

Jennifer Smith-Stead, Literacy Consultant

Copyright © 2001 by Tomie dePaola
All rights reserved.
This book, or parts thereof, may not be reproduced in any form
without permission in writing from the publisher,
G. P. Putnam's Sons, a division of Penguin Putnam Books for Young Readers,
345 Hudson Street, New York, NY 10014.
G. P. Putnam's Sons, Reg. U.S. Pat. & Tm. Off.
Published simultaneously in Canada.
Printed in Hong Kong by South China Printing Co. (1988) Ltd.
Designed by Sharon Murray Jacobs.
Text set in twenty-six point Worcester Round Medium.
The art for this book was created with transparent acrylics
on Fabriano 140 lb. handmade watercolor paper.
Library of Congress Cataloging-in-Publication Data
DePaola, Tomie. Meet the Barkers : Morgan and Moffat go to school / Tomie dePaola.
p. cm.
Summary: Bossy Moffie and her quiet twin brother Morgie both enjoy
starting school, especially getting gold stars and making new friends.
[1. First day of school—Fiction. 2. Schools—Fiction. 3. Brothers and sisters—Fiction.
4. Twins—Fiction. 5. Dogs—Fiction.] I. Title.
PZ7.D439   Mau 2001   [E]—dc21   00-055355   ISBN 0-399-23708-9
1 3 5 7 9 10 8 6 4 2
FIRST IMPRESSION

The Barkers were excited. The twins, Moffat and Morgan, were starting school. The Big Day was only a week away.

"Morgie," Moffie said. "We have to decide what we need for school."

"Later, Moffie," Morgie said. He was looking at the pictures in his dinosaur book.

"Now!" Moffie said.

"Okay," Morgie said. But he kept on looking at dinosaurs.

Morgie was used to Moffie being bossy and he didn't mind—*most* of the time.

The twins had been born on the same day, but Moffie had been born first.

"I'm the oldest, so I get to go first," Moffie always said.

Moffie was the first to walk. Morgie didn't mind. He just
watched where Moffie went, and walked when he was ready.

Moffie was the first to bark. Morgie didn't mind.
He just laughed, and barked when he was ready.

But Morgie was the first to be potty trained even though he was younger.

And Moffie *did* mind! Especially when she wet her pants. Morgie didn't tease her. But he knew that if he wet *his* pants, Moffie would have teased him.

"Morgan, Moffat! It's time to go shopping for school," Mama called.

"Hurry up, Morgie," Moffie said.

First they looked at backpacks.

Moffie knew exactly the one she wanted. A blue one with a kitten on it.

Morgie had a harder time. He looked at a blue one with a Tyrannosaurus rex on the flap and a red one with an Apatosaurus on the flap.

"Mine is blue," Moffie said, "so you take the red one."

"Okay," Morgie said.

"Now let's get our pencil boxes," Moffie said.
Moffie and Morgie wanted the same purple box.

"It's my favorite color," Moffie said.
"It's my favorite color too!" Morgie said.

"I changed my mind," Moffie said. "Pink is my favorite color."
"I still like purple," Morgie said.

Finally, it was the Big Day. Moffie couldn't wait to get to school. "Hurry up, Morgie! Hurry up!" The twins were going to be in the same class. Mama and Papa had asked the school to let them be together.

"Welcome, class," the teacher said. "I am Ms. Shepherd.
Let's go around the room and meet everyone."

Moffie was standing right next to the teacher.
"Let's start with you," Ms. Shepherd said.
"I'm Moffie." Before Morgie could say anything,
she said, "This is my brother, Morgie. We're twins."

After everyone had said their names, they all sat down.
"Boys and girls, today we are going to learn our colors,"
Ms. Shepherd said.

"I already know my colors," Moffie said, speaking right up.
"Red, orange, yellow, green, blue, violet, brown, and black."
"Very good, Moffie," Ms. Shepherd said.

Billy was sitting next to Morgie.

"Your sister is smart," he said.

"Yes, she is," Morgie said. "Do you want to see my dinosaur book?"

"Sure!" Billy said.

"How was your first day at school?" Mama asked.
"I got a gold star because I know all my colors," Moffie said.

"And I met a new friend. His name is Billy.
He likes dinosaurs too," Morgie told Mama.

The next day the twins got on the school bus.
"Hey, Morgie, sit with me!" Billy called from
the back of the bus.

Moffie sat in the first seat, right behind the driver.

"Today we are going to learn our numbers,"
Ms. Shepherd said.
    "I can count from one to ten," Moffie said. And she did.

Albert	Maria
Billy	Moffat ⭐⭐
Bobby	Morgan
Brendan	Sally
Jennifer	Sara
José	Tony
Katrina	

Moffie got another gold star.

On the playground, Morgie met Billy's friend Bobby.
"Can Bobby look at your dinosaur book?" Billy asked.
"Sure!" Morgie said.

All that week Moffie kept getting gold stars. Every time
Ms. Shepherd asked a question, Moffie jumped up with the answer.

On Thursday, Ms. Shepherd sat down next to Moffie.
"Moffie, it's wonderful that you know all the right answers.
But I need you to stop calling out every time I ask a question.
It's time to let the other children answer too."

"I'll try, Ms. Shepherd," Moffie said. *As long as they don't talk too long,* she thought.

"Now run along and play with your friends," Ms. Shepherd said.

But Moffie hadn't made any friends. She had been too busy getting gold stars.

She went to look for Morgie. *I'll get gold stars and Morgie can get friends,* she thought.

That afternoon, Moffie started to build a tower with wooden blocks. So did Sally.

I'm going to build the tallest tower, Moffie thought.

I'm going to build the tallest tower, Sally thought.

Suddenly all the blocks were used up. Moffie's tower and
Sally's tower were exactly the same size.

Moffie scowled. Sally scowled.
"What's the matter?" Morgie asked.

"I want to build the tallest tower," Moffie said.
"Me too," Sally said.

"Why don't you use all the blocks for one tower?
You can build a really tall tower together," Morgie said.

Moffie and Sally built the tallest tower in the classroom.
"That was fun, Moffie," Sally said.

"Yes. Tomorrow let's build the longest train!" Moffie said.

"Great! Do you want to sit together on the bus going home?" Sally asked.

"Sure!" Moffie said.

"Class, come and sit down. I'm going to read you a story about dinosaurs," Ms. Shepherd called out. "Does anyone know any dinosaurs' names?"

"I do," Morgie said, jumping up. "Tyrannosaurus rex, Apatosaurus, Triceratops, Stegosaurus, and Supersaurus!"

Morgie finished and the whole class clapped. Morgie
knew so many dinosaurs.

"That was wonderful, Morgie," Ms. Shepherd said.

Morgie grinned.

"What happened at school today?" Mama asked.
"How do you like school?" Papa asked.

"I got a gold star!" Morgie said.
"I got a best friend," Moffie said.
"We LOVE school!" they both said.